The RSPB
Bumper
Book of
Wildlife
Stories

First published 2013 by A & C Black,
an imprint of Bloomsbury Publishing Plc
50 Bedford Square
London WC1B 3DP

www.bloomsbury.com

HB ISBN 978-1-4081-7888-1
PB ISBN 978-1-4081-7889-8

A CIP catalogue for this book is available from the British Library.

MIX
Paper from
responsible sources
FSC® C008047

Printed and bound by in China by C&C Offset Printing Co.

1 3 5 7 9 10 8 6 4 2

The RSPB Bumper Book of Wildlife Stories

Pat Kelleher

STORIES ILLUSTRATED BY

Daniel Howarth

A & C BLACK
AN IMPRINT OF BLOOMSBURY
LONDON NEW DELHI NEW YORK SYDNEY

Contents

Mothers' Day 7
Find the ducklings 10

The World's Edge 11
Whose hole? 14

The Adventurous Little Blue Tit 15
Cliff dot-to-dot 18

Blackbird and the Ants 19
Ant fun 22

Outfoxed 23
Spot the difference 26

The Journey Home 27
Who goes where? 30

All Change 31
Bug bingo! 34

Mad Little Minnows 35
Fishy facts! 38

The Perfect Place 39
Vole hole maze 42

The Stoat who Gloated 43
Smell a slug maze 46

Bumblebee and the Night Shift. 47
Spot the difference 50

The Eagle's Search 51
Here comes Mum! 54

The Odd Couple. 55
Whose egg is it? 58

The Cricket who Landed in Trouble 59
Who's hiding here? 62

The King of All the Fishers. 63
Play time! 66

Oh Dear, Roe Deer 67
Puzzle fun 70

The Lonesome Pine 71
Spot the difference 74

The Blackbird and the Fox 75
Who is in the wood tonight? 78

The Mud Party 79
Spot the woodcocks! 82

The Moorhen and the Mud. 83
Spotty robins 86

The Sign of Spring 87
Dot-to-dot surprise! 90

The Hole Story 91
Bedtime for birds 94

More for You 95
Acknowledgements 96

Mothers' Day

Duckling loved his mother very much. He wanted to find her a present to show how much he loved her. He wandered away from the river and through a hedge and found himself in a field. "Maybe there is something here she might like?" he said.

"Ouch! Watch where you're stepping!" said a voice. Duckling looked down. There, lying in a shallow hole by the hedge was a furry little creature with long ears. It was Leveret. Leveret loved her mother, too. She couldn't wait to grow up into a hare like her mum.

"Sorry," said Duckling. "I didn't see you."

"That's the idea," said Leveret. "My mother loves me so much she hides me here. It keeps me safe from animals that would gobble me up."

"Don't you have any brothers or sisters? I have lots," said Duckling proudly.

"I do have a brother and sister!" said Leveret. "I just don't know where Mum keeps them," she added quietly. "But they're somewhere in the field. Mum keeps us in different places, so that we don't get gobbled up together."

"My mum never leaves me alone," said Duckling. "When we were a day old, she took us all out of the nest and down to the river. We spend hours every day dabbling for bits of weed, seeds and the odd crunchy insect to eat."

"Your mum makes you find your own food?" said Leveret, hardly able to believe her very big ears. "My mum never does that. She comes to me several times a day to give me a drink of milk."

"Do keep the noise down," said a little voice from above. "I'm trying to eat."

Duckling and Leveret looked up into the hedge to see a caterpillar sat on a leaf.

"Do you have a mother?" said Leveret.

"What's a mother?" said Caterpillar.

"Don't you know?" said Duckling and Leveret together.

"I know that I hatched from an egg and all I want to do is eat, eat, eat!"

"Do you have brothers and sisters?" asked Duckling.

"Well, there are other caterpillars here too. Are they brothers and sisters? I don't know. I'm too busy eating to find out," said Caterpillar. "All the food I ever want is right here. I don't have to find it and nobody has to bring it to me."

There was a loud quacking from the hedge.

"Uh-oh, it's Mum," said Duckling.

"There's my darling!" said Mother Duck. "I thought something had gobbled you up. I was so worried!"

Mother Hare came bounding up. "I heard you squeal! I thought something had gobbled you up," she said to Leveret.

"It was an accident," said Leveret. "Duckling stood on me."

"Children, they're such a worry, aren't they?" said Mother Hare to Mother Duck.

"I was only looking for a present for you," said Duckling.

"The best present you could give me is to be safe!" said Mother Duck to Duckling. "After all, you're my darling little ducky-wuckling, aren't you?"

"Aaaw, Mum, that's so embarrassing!" said Duckling as Mother Duck led him and his brothers and sisters back to the river.

"Peace and quiet at last!" said Caterpillar, talking with his mouth full because he didn't have a mum to tell him not to do that. "Now, where was I? Oh yes. Juicy leaves. Nom nom nom..."

Find the ducklings

Can Mother Duck warn all her ducklings before the pike eats them? Lead her round the pond so that she can find all of them before the pike does!

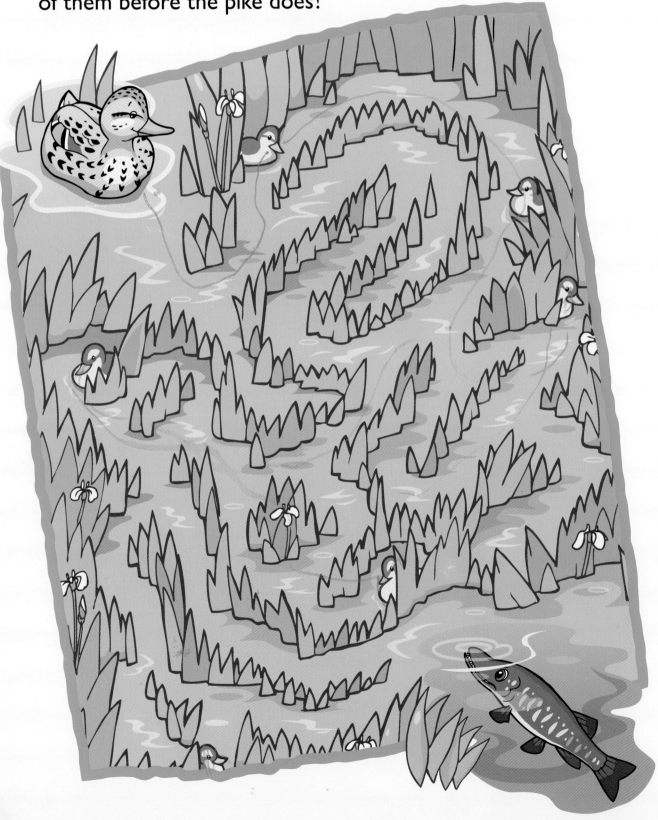

The World's Edge

One night, in the warm end of a tunnel, Mother Badger gave birth to two little babies. They were cute and pink and their eyes were still shut. Mother Badger loved them and licked them and called them her own. They slept and drank milk from Mother Badger and drank milk and slept, for they were too small to do anything else.

Every day, they grew a bit more. Their eyes opened. Their silver fur started to grow with just the faintest of two black stripes on their faces. Even though they looked the same, Mother Badger knew they were as different as the black and white stripes on their heads. One was a brother. One was a sister.

Deep underground, their little, dark world was full of straw and earth.

Sometimes, a strange glow would appear at the other end of the tunnel.

Every now and again, Mother Badger would wriggle out of the small, cosy chamber and go off up the tunnel. But Brother and Sister Badger never felt scared.

"Where does she go?" asked Sister Badger. "What does she do?"

"It doesn't matter,' said Brother Badger with a yawn. "She always comes back."

"But I want to know!" said Sister Badger.

So when Mother Badger came back they both drank some milk, cuddled up to her again, and Sister Badger asked, "Where do you go?"

"Out" said Mother Badger.

"What do you do?"

"Things," said Mother Badger. "When it is time for you to know I will tell you," she said kindly. "For now you must always stay here below, where it is dark and warm and safe."

And Mother Badger loved them and licked them and called them her own. Brother Badger was happy.

But Sister Badger was not.

"What did she mean? If we are below, that means that there must be something above. But what?" she asked, as Mother Badger slept.

Brother Badger yawned. "Go to sleep," he said, turning over. They were growing so much there wasn't much room left in their cosy little chamber.

"And what's that?" said Sister Badger, unable to sleep.

Brother Badger opened an eye.

The glow filled the tunnel again.

"It's the not-dark. It comes and goes," he mumbled. "It's nothing."

But Sister Badger wanted to see for herself. "Come on," she said, pushing her brother into the tunnel.

They crept up the tunnel towards the glow. It seemed to be a bright, round, circle. Squinting their eyes at the brightness, they shuffled nearer.

Suddenly, Brother Badger tumbled forwards and vanished into the light with a cry.

It was as if his whole world had disappeared. The earth, the walls, the roof and the dark were gone. The hot brightness all around him hurt his eyes so he couldn't see. He snuffled round in a circle, not sure where to go or what to do.

In the tunnel entrance, Sister Badger felt scared. It was her fault that Brother Badger had fallen out of the world.

She called out blindly into the bright beyond, "Brother Badger, Brother Badger where are you?"

Brother Badger heard her calling.

He couldn't see, but he followed the sound of her voice until their snouts met and he felt the comforting walls of the tunnel close about him again.

Trembling, they crept back down into the dark together until they were snug and safe against Mother Badger once more.

When Mother Badger woke up she turned to them. "My own," she said. "You are growing up and will soon be too old for milk. It is time for me to teach you about Outside."

"No!" gasped Sister Badger.

"It hurts my eyes!" cried Brother Badger.

And Mother Badger knew they had been outside. She sighed.

Then Mother Badger loved them and licked them and called them her own.

"You went out in the light," she said. "Badgers live in the dim and the dark. We never leave our home by day." And she led the way up the tunnel.

This time there was no fierce glow.

"See?" said Mother Badger as she stepped outside. "This is night, when the outside is as dark as a badger's home."

Sister and Brother Badger tiptoed out of the tunnel. This time the world didn't fall away. The light didn't hurt. Instead, the moon bathed them in a silver light that was as soft and gentle as the silver of Mother Badger's fur.

And that night and for many nights afterwards, Brother and Sister Badger played happily in the moonlight while Mother Badger looked on.

Whose hole?

The badger, fox and rabbit all live in holes underground.
Can you lead them to their homes?

A badger's home is called a sett. A fox's home is called an earth. A rabbit's home is called a burrow.

The Adventurous Little
Blue Tit

Little Blue Tit looked at the trees and bushes all around. He knew this world. But beyond the trees and bushes, something twinkled and flashed in the light.

"What's that?" he asked his mum.

Mother Blue Tit looked into the distance and said, "Oh, that? That's the sea. You don't want to bother with that."

"The sea!" said Little Blue Tit with a sigh.

It looked so shiny and sparkly. It looked much more interesting than trees and bushes. "I want to go to the sea!" he said.

"Why would you want to do that, my little feather dumpling?" asked Mother Blue Tit. "You've got all you need right here. You have trees and bushes to live in, and caterpillars to eat. What more do you want?"

"Adventure!" said Little Blue Tit.

"Oh, well, if that's what you want, go to next door's garden when the cat's out. That's adventure enough for me!" she said.

Little Blue Tit didn't say anything. He was too busy gazing at the sparkling sea.

The next day Gull flew past.

"Excuse me," called Little Blue Tit. "I want to run away to sea!"

"Do you, now?" said Gull. "You don't look like a sea bird to me."

"I can be," said Little Blue Tit. "Ahar!" he added, and, "Yo-Ho-Ho!"

"Well, it's ahar-d life being a sea bird," said Gull.

"I can do it!" said Little Blue Tit.

"Let's Yo-Ho-Hope so," said Gull.

The sea was a lot further away than it looked but soon they were flying out over the cliffs and across the big, blue waves.

"Wheeee!" cried Little Blue Tit. But by now his little wings were very tired. "I need to sit on a branch and get my strength back," he said. He couldn't see any branches. In fact, he couldn't see any trees.

"When I'm tired I sit on the sea," said Gull, "but then I have webbed feet to help me paddle."

"I don't," said Little Blue Tit, sadly. "I have little claws for gripping branches."

"Well, sometimes I sit on the cliff," said Gull.

So Little Blue Tit sat on a narrow rocky ledge on the crowded sea cliff. "I'm hungry!" he said to a razorbill sitting next to him. "What do you eat?"

"I eat fish from the sea."

"Oh," said Little Blue Tit unhappily. "I don't know how to catch fish. I can only catch caterpillars."

The wind blew. It was wet and cold.

"Where's your nest?" he asked Razorbill, shivering.

"Nest?" said Razorbill. "We sleep on cliff ledges. That's what salty sea birds do."

"Oh," said Little Blue Tit. Being a sea bird didn't seem like much fun any more. "I'd rather be snug in my tree hole, where it's warm and dry," he said as it started to rain. "I think I want to go Yo-Ho-Home."

So he flew back to his mother, his trees and his bushes. He much preferred adventure in the high trees than on the high seas.

Cliff dot-to-dot

Join the dots to find which bird is on the cliffs. Do you know what it is? If you are not sure, turn the page upside down to find out.

Colour in the picture once you have joined the dots.

A razorbill

Blackbird and the Ants

Blackbird was building her nest in a hawthorn bush. "It's going to be the biggest, best nest ever!" she said. She was looking on the ground for some dried grass when she saw a small wood ant carrying a pine needle.

"What are you doing?" she asked.

"Building a nest," it said.

"It must be a very tiny nest," said Blackbird. "What a cute little ant, building a teeny-weeny nest for its itty-bitty ant eggs. Bless!"

"If you say so," said the wood ant. "But I must be on my way, I have work to do." And it carried on its way.

Looking for soft moss to line her nest, Blackbird saw another small wood ant carrying a piece of grass.

"And what are you doing?" she asked.

"Building a nest," it said.

Blackbird laughed. "That's so sweet! Another cute little ant building another teeny-weeny nest for its itty-bitty ant eggs. Aaaah!"

"If you say so," said the wood ant. "But I must be on my way, I have work to do." And off it went.

"There," said Blackbird, lining her nest with soft moss. "Finished. I don't think I'll see a better nest. I certainly won't see a bigger one," she said, remembering the ants.

She saw another small wood ant, carrying a leaf.

"And what are you doing?" she said with a smile. "As if I couldn't guess."

"Building a nest," it said.

"Oooh!" said Blackbird. "So many little ants building teeny-weeny nests for their itty-bitty ant eggs. That's adorable."

"If you say so," said the wood ant. "But I must be on my way, I have work to do." And off it went.

"I must see what their darling little nests look like," said Blackbird, so she followed the small ant. She saw lots of other ants carrying pine needles, bits of grass, and leaves. "Why, there must be lots and lots of tiny little ants' nests," she said.

Then, in the middle of a clearing, she saw a large mound of pine needles, grass and leaves.

"Oh," said Blackbird.

The ants weren't making lots of little teeny-weeny nests – they were making one huge nest instead. Blackbird's nest wasn't the biggest and best in the wood after all.

This was much bigger than hers. In fact, it was even bigger than she was. It seemed to be moving, as thousands of ants swarmed all over it, building and mending.

"Do you like our nest?" said one ant.

"But it's so… big!" said Blackbird.

"We've been working together to build it," said another.

"We have the biggest nest in the whole wood!" said all the ants together. "Just because we're small doesn't mean that we can't build something big."

"If you say so," said Blackbird in a small voice. "Excuse me, I must be on my way." And off she flew back to her nest, feeling very foolish indeed.

Ant fun

The ants are busy collecting things to build their nest. Can you count all the ants on this page? Turn the page upside down to see if you are right.

Answer: There are ⬜15⬜ ants.

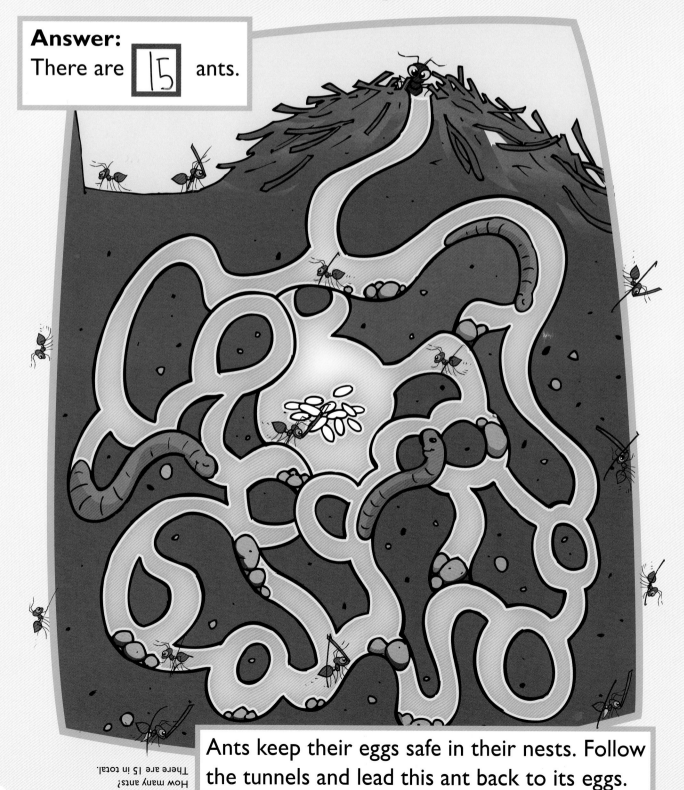

Ants keep their eggs safe in their nests. Follow the tunnels and lead this ant back to its eggs.

How many ants?
There are 15 in total.

22

Outfoxed

Fox was cunning and clever. The other woodland animals didn't like him at all. But he didn't mind. He liked them. Well, he liked creeping up on them and eating them for lunch, which is not quite the same thing.

One day, Fox came to the edge of the wood. There he saw a large rabbit. It was sitting up on its hind legs in the middle of the field, right out in the open, without a care in the world.

"This is going to be the easiest dinner I've ever caught," said Fox, licking his lips as he crept through the meadow towards it.

"Don't think I can't see you," said the big rabbit loudly. "You're not as sneaky as you think, friend."

"How dare you!" said Fox. "I'm the cleverest and best animal in the wood. I am sharp of eye and keen of snout, smart of brain and fast of foot and no one is clever enough to be friends with me!"

"No one is stupid enough, you mean," said the big rabbit. "You'd eat them soon as look at them, you would."

"You know, for a rabbit you've got a very big mouth," snapped Fox.

"That's because I'm not a rabbit," it said.

"But you've got big ears," said Fox.

"You've got a bushy tail, but that doesn't make you a squirrel, does it? Look at me; I have bigger ears than a rabbit. I'm larger than a rabbit and I have bigger back legs than a rabbit. And do you know why?" it said. "Because I'm a hare, that's why! Fancy not knowing that – and you call yourself clever?"

"Doesn't matter what you're called," said Fox crossly. "You're just lunch to me."

"There you go again," said Hare. "I'm only lunch if you can catch me."

"Oh, I'll catch you all right," said Fox. "I'm sharp of eye and keen of snout, fast of foot…"

"Yes, yes, yes," said Hare wearily.

"So you said."

"Right, just for that I won't give you a head start," said Fox.

"Don't need one," said Hare. "Bye!" And off he shot across the field.

Fox chased after him but Hare raced away on his big back legs. Fox soon had to give up. He would never catch up. Hare was just too fast.

Hare sat up on his back legs again, keeping an eye on Fox, and called out from across the field.

"You may be the best at what you do," he said, "but I'm the best at what I do – outrunning you! Why, you might even say I'm outstanding in my field!"

And because Hare was out, standing in his field, he could always see Fox coming. Fox could never creep up on him. And Fox, being cunning and clever, knew that. So Fox did what he was best at – he crept away, but this time hungry and with his tail between his legs.

Spot the difference

These two pictures of Fox chasing Hare look the same, but there are six differences. Can you spot them?

The Journey Home

When Swallow first flew to Africa with all the other swallows, it was very exciting. Africa was big. Africa was hot. Africa had lots and lots of insects to eat.

There were lions and elephants, giraffes and zebras. Insects buzzed around each one. There were insects everywhere. Swallows darted happily about, snatching them out of the air. Swallow thought it was the best place in the world. He was well fed, warm and happy.

But one day, he began to think about his little nest in a barn far, far away. Swallow felt homesick.

"I want to go home," he said.

All around him, other swallows felt the same. They were beginning to dream of their own little nests, too.

No one knew who started it, but the word went round, from swallow to swallow. "It is time. Pass it on. It is time."

Soon every swallow knew.

It was time. Time to go home again.

Day after day, small flocks of swallow friends and families took to the air. They flew round the great grassy plains.

They flew over the big rivers, as if to say goodbye. Then they turned north and flew away.

On and on, over the great, green forests of central Africa, the flocks flew. They stopped only to sleep in the trees, or in tall reeds on the banks of rivers.

Then one day the great, green forests ended and they left them far behind.

"Are we nearly there, yet?" asked Swallow.

"No," said an older swallow.

Swallow sighed, for stretching ahead, as far he could see, was the desert.

Swallow didn't feel quite so happy or quite so well fed any more. His wings ached and he felt very thirsty. Only the thought of his little nest kept him going.

On and on over the hot, baking sands of North Africa they flew. They stopped only to drink water from tiny lakes called oases and to rest in the palm trees that grew round them.

Then one day the desert ended and they left it far behind.

"Are we nearly there, yet?" asked Swallow.

"No."

For stretching ahead of them for as far as they could see was the sea.

On and on over the waves they flew until they saw land.

"Are we nearly there yet?" asked Swallow.

"No."

For rising high in front of them they saw snow-topped mountains. Up and over they flew, stopping only to shelter in the rocks from the great cold winds.

Then one day the mountains fell away and they left them far behind.

"Are we nearly there yet?" asked Swallow.

"Nearly."

For spread out before them were fields. Green fields, yellow fields, large fields and little fields.

Swallow was tired. His wings still ached. But he was happy. He was almost home.

Then big falcons with sharp talons and hooked beaks saw them coming. One by one, they swooped down. They picked swallows out of the air for lunch, just like the swallows snatched up insects. Swallow flew as hard as he could and didn't look back.

Soon they left the falcons far behind.

On and on they flew. Then one day, spread out below him, Swallow saw places he knew. There was the wood. There was the meadow. There was the stream. And there! There was the barn, his barn, where he had hatched last summer.

His long journey was over.

He was home at last.

Who goes where?

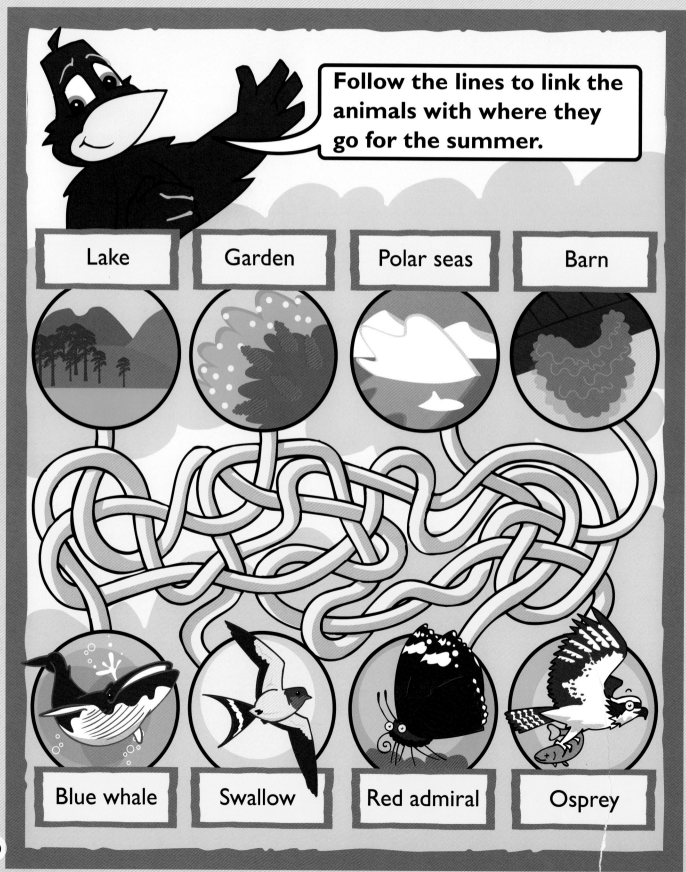

Follow the lines to link the animals with where they go for the summer.

Lake Garden Polar seas Barn

Blue whale Swallow Red admiral Osprey

All Change

Peacock Caterpillar lived in the nettles with his friends. They spent all day eating.

"There's nothing better than being a caterpillar," said Caterpillar. "And there's nothing better to eat than nettle leaves!"

It was just as well he liked nettles, for he had nettles for breakfast, nettles for dinner and nettles for tea.

"I need my food," he said. "I am a growing caterpillar after all."

And Caterpillar did grow. He grew so big and fat that his skin became too small for him. He had to wriggle out of it, like squirming out of a jumper that is too small for you. His new skin was nice and soft and stretchy.

"Look at my new skin," said Caterpillar to his friends, but there was no-one to admire him. "Hello?" he called through a mouthful of nettle.

But nobody answered. His friends had all vanished.

"Your friends have all gone," said a ladybird.

"Gone? Gone where?" asked Caterpillar.

"Well, some got so fat and juicy that cuckoos ate them," said the ladybird. "And others grew up."

"Really?" said Caterpillar. "Hoorah! More nettles for me then!" he said, scoffing up another leaf. He didn't really miss his friends. All he cared about was eating.

Soon, he began to feel full.

"Phew! I couldn't eat another bite! I don't think I can face another nettle leaf," he sighed. He wobbled off through the grass to look for something that wasn't a nettle plant.

He found a holly bush. As he climbed it, he found his skin getting harder and tighter until it was tricky to move at all.

"I'll rest on this branch," he panted. Using his special caterpillar bottom, he spun a short rope made of caterpillar silk. Now he could hang safely from the branch, away from anything that might want to eat a nice juicy caterpillar. "I'll just have a little nap," he said.

And he fell asleep in his hard, tight skin.

When Caterpillar woke up, it felt like he was tangled up in a blanket.

"Help! Help!" he cried. He kicked and then he was free. But he felt wet, as if he had just climbed out of a bath.

"How odd," he said. And he spread his wings out to dry. "Aah! Wings! What happened to all my lovely legs?" he cried.

"You've grown up!" said a butterfly. "You're not Peacock Caterpillar any more. You're Peacock Butterfly."

It was true. He had changed while he was asleep. He didn't feel big and wobbly any more. He felt as light as a feather. And to prove it he flapped his wings and floated into the air.

"I feel hungry," he said. "But I've gone right off nettles. What can I eat?"

His new friend stuck her long tongue into a pretty purple flower and sucked a sweet juice through it, like a straw.

So he tried it too.

"Ooh, that is so much better than nettles!" he said. "I think I'm going to like being a butterfly even more than being a caterpillar."

And he did.

Bug bingo!

Go out into the garden or a park and see how many of these creatures you can tick off.

White butterfly

Colourful butterfly

Caterpillar

Ant

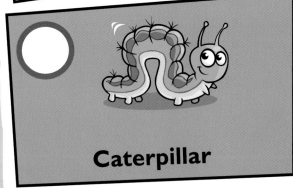

Ladybird

Beetle

Bee or wasp

Greenfly

When you have ticked all the boxes, you can shout BINGO!

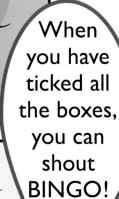

Mad Little Minnows

Minnow and his three minnow mates were the fastest fish in the river. Whatever Minnow did, his minnow mates followed. Minnow zipped through the water, swimming in the sunshine so his silver scales shone. And his minnow mates followed.

The next day, Minnow dived down to the bottom. He slipped under boulders, finding scraps to eat. And his minnow mates followed.

"Isn't this fun?" said Minnow.

"Yes," said his three mates.

Merry little minnows.

The next day, Minnow twisted in the currents catching tiny shrimps to eat. And his minnow mates followed.

"Isn't this fun?" said Minnow.

"Yes," said his three mates.

Munching little minnows.

Minnow dashed and darted round a big old fish. And his minnow mates followed.

"Watch where you're going!" called Tench. "Or you'll get into trouble!"

"You are one, we are – um – many. Together we have lots of eyes to watch out for trouble," said Minnow. "And if we see it coming – zip! We dash away!"

"I wouldn't count on that," said Tench.

Minnow couldn't count at all. But it didn't worry him. He was a fish. What did he have to count?

"Remember to stay out of the shadows where the long weeds grow," said Tench.

Minnow didn't remember at all. But it didn't worry him. He was a fish. What did he have to remember?

"Isn't this fun?" said Minnow.

"Yes," said his three mates.

Mischievous little minnows.

The next day, Minnow swam near the shadows where the long weeds grew, looking for morsels to eat. And his minnow mates followed.

"Isn't this fun?" said Minnow.

"Yes," said his two mates.

Mad little minnows.

The next day, Minnow swam into the shadows where long weeds grew and then he swam right out again. And his minnow mate followed.

"Isn't this fun?" said Minnow.

"Yes," said his mate.

Mistaken little minnows.

The next day, Minnow swam right through the shadows where the long weeds grew and out the other side again. And his minnow mate followed.

"Isn't this fun?" said Minnow.

But there was no one left to answer.

Missing little minnows.

The next day, Minnow swam through the shadows where the long weeds grew, out of the other side and back the way he came again.

"Isn't this fun?" said Minnow.

"YES!" said a voice from the shadows where the long weeds grew.

Out shot Pike with his big, sharp teeth. Mouth-watering little minnow! Nom, nom, nom!

"This isn't fun!" cried Minnow as he zigged and he zagged and Pike snipped and snapped. But Minnow was the fastest fish in the river and he got clean away.

The next day, Minnow made some new friends. He didn't know how many. Minnow couldn't count at all. But it didn't worry him. He was a fish. What did he have to count?

"This is fun," said Minnow.

"Yes," said his new friends.

Minnow swam by the shadows where long weeds grew. Minnow didn't remember them at all. But it didn't worry him. He was a fish. What did he have to remember?

So the next day, Minnow swam into the shadows where the long weeds grew. And his new friends followed…

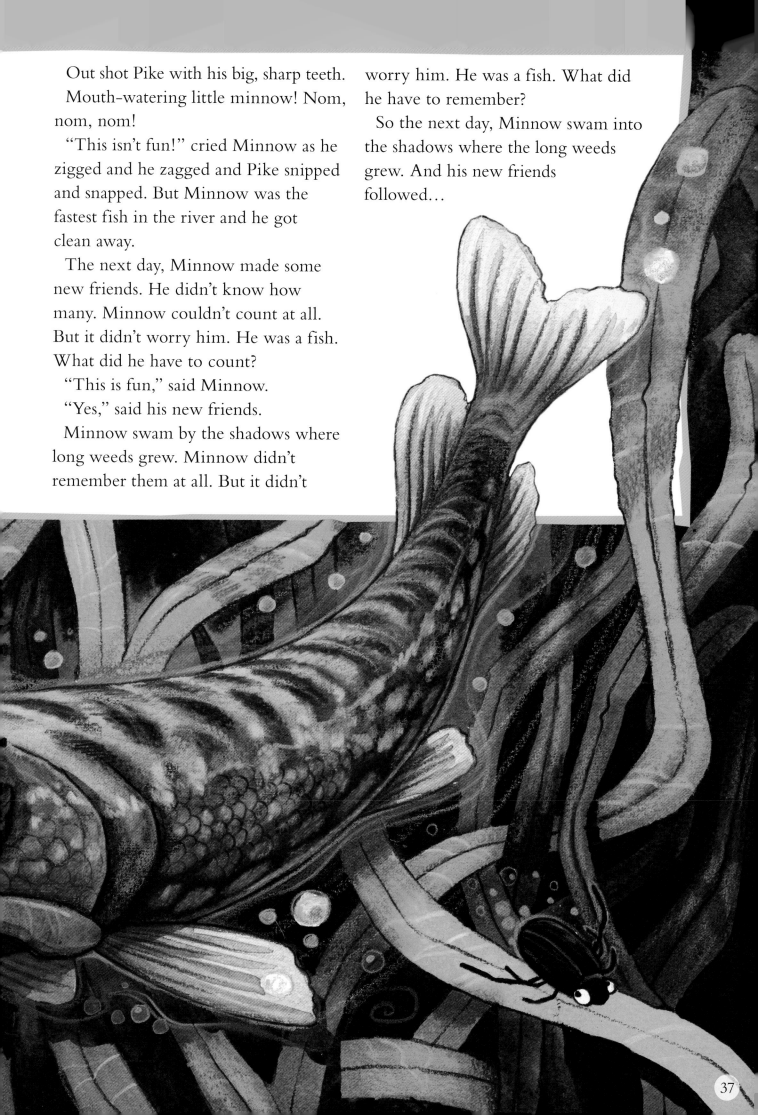

Fishy facts!

Minnow can't see who's hiding in the reeds. Can you? Join the dots to find out.

A group of birds together is called a flock. But a group of fishes together is called a shoal.

Why don't you colour in the picture after you've joined the dots?

A pike

The Perfect Place

There was a story going round. The animals whispered it to each other in the grass and up the trees, by the river and on the breeze. There was only one problem. Each animal was sure the story was just about them.

"Have you heard?" said Water Vole. "Over the hill the Two-Legs have made a special place just for water voles to live happily ever after!"

"Water voles, are you sure?" said Lapwing. "I heard it was lapwings!"

"You must have heard wrong," said Kingfisher. "My cousin's best friend's brother told me that it was totally for kingfishers, so there!"

"Your cousin's best friend's brother must have cloth ears," said Partridge, "because my auntie's uncle's niece said it was for partridges."

The animals began to argue amongst themselves.

"Enough!" cried Water Vole. "I shall set out and see if the tale is true," he said, "for if anyone deserves a special place to live, it is me."

Over the hill, it was just as he had heard. The tale was true.

There was just one problem – everybody else thought so, too.

"What are you doing here?" Water Vole asked Lapwing. "This place is for water voles! Look, the Two-Legs clean the river and fill it with tasty water plants. This is made for water voles, I tell you."

"You're wrong," said Lapwing. "Look, the Two-Legs have left squelchy, wet grass and juicy grubs in the meadow by the river. This is for lapwings."

"Lapwings, pah!" said Kingfisher. "It's quite clear this place is for kingfishers. See how the trees overhang the river. The Two-Legs keep it full of fish."

"Go away, all of you," cried Partridge, bursting out of the long grass. "This is my place! This isn't for the likes of you! Look at all the long grass and seedy-seeds the Two-Legs give me. This is a partridge place – for partridges."

And the animals began arguing all over again.

Then a little voice piped up.

"It doesn't seem like a happy place at all if we're all arguing," said Water Vole.

"Yes, why would the Two-Legs make a place like this?" said Lapwing.

"I don't know," said Partridge. "But there is something in the grass. It might give us a clue."

It was a big wooden thing on a tree trunk.

The animals looked up at it.

It just stood there.

"Well, you can't live in it," said Water Vole.

"You can't eat it," said Lapwing.

"You can't even fish from it," said Kingfisher.

"Or hide in it," said Partridge. "Whatever is it for?"

"It's… it's… for making friends," said Water Vole slowly. They all looked at him.

"Well, we're not arguing now, are we?"

"But we can't all be right!" said Kingfisher. "Can we?"

"Perhaps we can," said Lapwing.

"It does seem to be a nice, safe place. A place for everyone," said Partridge. "Friends?"

"Friends!" they decided.

And they went off to enjoy their new homes – no problem at all.

The big wooden thing watched them go.

It didn't do anything else at all.

It just said: **Nature Reserve**.

Vole hole maze

This water vole can't remember how to get back to its hole in the bank. Can you help it to find its way home?

The Stoat who Gloated

If there was one thing that Stoat loved more than anything else, it was himself. He often went down to the pond so he could look at himself in the water.

"Morning, Stoat," said Hedgehog. Stoat looked down his nose at him.

"Are you talking to me?" he said.

"Yes," said Hedgehog in a small voice.

"Well, don't," said Stoat. "You're not clever enough to talk to me. I have five keen senses. With your poor eyesight you can't even see how splendid I am." And with his nose in the air he strode past on his way to the pond.

"My eyesight may be poor," said Hedgehog, "but I have a very keen sense of smell instead and I can smell trouble."

But Stoat had gone.

Then Stoat came across Owl.

"Good morning, Stoat," said Owl.

"Are you talking to me?" said Stoat. "Well, don't. You're not clever enough to talk to me. I have five keen senses. You have no nose and can't catch the sweet smell of success that follows me." And he strode past with his nose in the air.

"My sense of smell may be poor, but I have very good hearing instead," said Owl. "And it sounds like you'll come a cropper one day."

But Stoat had gone.

"Hello, Stoat," said Rabbit.

"Are you talking to me?" asked Stoat. "Well, don't. You're not clever enough to talk to me. I have five keen senses. You may have paws but you can't touch me for sheer brilliance." And he strode past with his nose in the air.

"My touch may be poor, but I have a very good sense of taste," said Rabbit, "and one day you'll bite off more than you can chew."

But Stoat had gone.

"Is that you, Stoat?" asked Mole.

"Are you talking to me?" asked Stoat. "Well, don't. You're not clever enough to talk to me. I have five keen senses. You have a tiny mouth and eat worms. I have much better taste than to talk to you." And he strode past with his nose in the air.

"My taste may be poor, but I have a very good sense of touch," said Mole, "and I have a feeling this won't end well."

Stoat arrived at the pond and was looking forward to admiring himself.

"Hello, Stoat," said a voice.

"Are you talking to me?" asked Stoat, looking around, but he couldn't see anyone. "Who's there?" he asked.

"I thought you had five keen senses?" said the voice.

Stoat turned round and round. "Who are you?" he cried. He became so dizzy he fell into the pond with a great big splash. He didn't look so clever now. He felt wet, his wet fur smelled horrible, he looked a mess and, on top of all that, he heard the voice again.

"Why, I'm Flea," it said. "I live on your back and if I hear you boast again I shall bite you."

Well, from that day to this Stoat scratched and scritched trying to catch Flea, but he never could. He didn't dare boast ever again, just in case Flea bit him.

Smell a slug maze

Can you help the hedgehog smell his way to a slug dinner?

Bumblebee and the Night Shift

Bumblebee loved flowers. You just couldn't keep her away from them. Every day, she flew from flower to flower, tasting their nectar.

Other minibeasts liked the flowers too. The pretty butterflies flitted from one to the other, giggling and gossiping, sipping the nectar with their long tongues.

"Excuse me. Bee at work. Just checking the nectar," said Bumblebee, trying to squeeze past.

The butterflies flittered off, giggling to each other.

"Tut, butterflies!" said Bee. She sucked away at the nectar. "Hmm, this is nice."

That evening, Bumblebee stopped for a rest on her way back to her nest. She had just settled in the grass near a plant when she caught a flash of yellow and black out of the corner of her eye. Yellow and black meant danger so she looked again.

"Wait a minute. I'm yellow. I'm black. I'm dangerous, too!" she said. She didn't feel quite so worried when she saw a bit of plant move.

But it wasn't a bit of plant at all. It was something pretending to look like it.

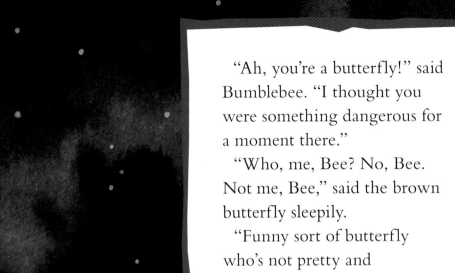

"Ah, you're a butterfly!" said Bumblebee. "I thought you were something dangerous for a moment there."

"Who, me, Bee? No, Bee. Not me, Bee," said the brown butterfly sleepily.

"Funny sort of butterfly who's not pretty and bright like the others," said Bumblebee, shaking her head as she went off to bed.

The next day Bumblebee spent all day flying from flower to flower. In the evening, she met the brown butterfly again, sleeping hidden against the plant.

"Why are you sleeping when you should be out collecting nectar?" said Bumblebee.

"Who, me, Bee? No, Bee. Not me, Bee," said the brown butterfly sleepily.

"Funny sort of butterfly, sleeping all day," said Bumblebee shaking her head as she flew off to bed.

The next day, Bumblebee flew from flower to flower and that evening met the sleeping brown butterfly again.

"You should have been out flying among the flowers in the sunshine," said Bumblebee.

"Who, me, Bee? No, Bee. Not me, Bee," said the brown butterfly sleepily.

"Funny sort of butterfly who doesn't like sunshine. Never

mind. It's too late now. The flowers are shutting for the night. You missed them all," said Bumblebee shaking her head as she flew off to bed.

"Tut, butterflies!" she said.

As the sun went down, the brown butterfly stretched its wings and woke up.

"Butterfly, indeed. Funny sort of bumblebee who's never heard of moths," said Moth.

Every night, Moth opened his brown wings out, showing the yellow and black on his second pair of wings hidden underneath. Then he flew off in the dark, following the strong,

sweet smells of the night flowers.

"Tut, bumblebees!" said Moth. "Funny sort of bumblebee that doesn't know you can collect nectar at night, too! Well, she can keep the days. She's welcome to them. I'll stick to nights."

And so he did.

Spot the difference

Can you see seven differences between the two pictures?

The Eagle's Search

Young Eagle was alone. He flew high over the mountains from place to place, from highland to moorland, looking for a place to live.

"One day," he said, "I will find a home."

He would see valleys full of red deer.

"This is the place for me," he'd say.

Or he would spot mountain hares with his keen eyes.

"I can live in a place like this," he'd say.

Or he would hear the call of wild grouse from the heather.

"This is a place to call home," he'd say.

And he would snatch up a grouse from the heather or a hare from the moor to eat.

But each time he would hear the cries of two bigger eagles.

"What are you doing here?" they would call. "This is our glen, our home!"

"But it is summer and there is food for all of us," said Eagle.

"You may stay to rest your wings and fill your belly," they told him. "That has been the way of the eagle for longer than eagles can remember. But this is our home, our glen, our food and you must move on."

He would watch the eagle pair fly off together, and he would feel more lonely and lost than before.

On and on he flew, looking for a valley of his own. But whenever he saw other eagle pairs in the distance they called out, warning him off.

"What are you doing here?" they said. "This is our glen, our home. Be gone and find your own! Winter is coming and there isn't food for us all here!"

Tired and hungry, he was about to give up when he found a glen. He saw a great herd of red deer. He spotted mountain hares and heard the calls of wild grouse.

"There is plenty of food here," said Eagle happily. "I have found my home."

But then he heard a familiar cry and saw the shape of an eagle circling down towards him.

"It's all right. I'll go!" he said sadly. "It's just that it's such a nice valley and I was hungry and tired. I suppose your mate is coming to help chase me away?" he said.

"No," said the female eagle. "I'm all alone, too."

"You are?"

"This is my home, my glen, but I can't build a nest by myself," she said. "Will you stay and help me?"

"Yes!" he said.

The two eagles gathered up sticks and collected bits of heather and sheep's wool to make the nest nice and soft inside. Then on the highest mountain ledge they could find, they began to build a nest. Together.

A month later, their first chicks hatched.

Eagle was happy. He was no longer alone.

"This is our glen, our home now," he said proudly.

And it was.

Here comes Mum!

Join the dots and see who is coming to land at the nest.

Swap the letters round to find out what Mum and her chicks are.

LEGAE

The Odd Couple

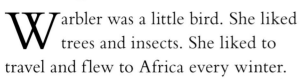

Warbler was a little bird. She liked trees and insects. She liked to travel and flew to Africa every winter.

Bittern was a big bird. He liked muddy reedbeds, fish and frogs and liked to stay in the nature reserve where he was.

They were as different as chalk and cheese.

One day, Warbler flew over the reedbed on her way to some trees. Bittern flew up out of the marsh on his way to more reeds. They nearly crashed into each other.

Warbler had never seen a bittern before.

"Gosh, you're big!" said Warbler.

Bittern had never seen a warbler before.

"Aye," said Bittern. "And you're little."

"So where are you going?" asked Warbler. "Perhaps we can fly together?"

"Only to the reeds over there," said Bittern.

"Oh!" she said, disappointed. "I don't do reeds. I like trees. You could come with me if you like," said Warbler.

"I don't think so," sniffed Bittern. "I don't like to leave my reeds."

"Why, you and your reeds! You're just an old stick in the mud!" she said.

"Charming!" huffed Bittern.

"Well, how do you know that you don't like trees if you've never tried them? Come on. It'll be fun."

Bittern shrugged. "Whatever."

So Bittern flew off with Warbler to try the trees.

Warbler's little feet let her grip on to the smallest of branches and her little beak let her peck up the juiciest of insects.

But Bittern's feet were big and clumsy and it was hard to hold on. And his big beak was too long to pick up tiny bugs.

"I want my reeds," he said sourly.

"Oh, you!" chirped Warbler.

So Warbler flew off with Bittern to try the reeds.

Bittern's big feet let him walk across the soggy marsh without sinking and his long beak let him pluck out the juiciest fish.

But Warbler found it hard to hold on to the swaying reeds with her little feet, and her small beak was too short to help her catch fish.

"We don't seem to have anything in common," said Warbler sadly.

A hunting bird flew low over the reeds

looking for prey.

"Danger!" they both cried. They both knew that birds with hooked beaks meant trouble.

"Quick," said Bittern. "I'm big, you're small. Hide under me."

"But how will you hide?" she asked as she huddled between his legs.

"Don't you worry about that," he said. He stretched his neck up and pointed his beak into the sky. Then he began to sway in the breeze. With his shape and special colours, he looked just like all the other reeds in the muddy marsh.

The hunter flew right by and didn't even see them. They were safe.

"Thank you," said Warbler.

"So," said Bittern. "Maybe I'm not such an old stick in the mud after all, then?"

"No," chirped Warbler, "but you can look like an old stick in the mud – and thank goodness for that!"

After that, the two became firm friends and used to visit each other often, even though Bittern could still eat no bugs and Warbler could eat no fish.

Whose egg is it?

Follow each line to find out what creature these eggs will turn into.

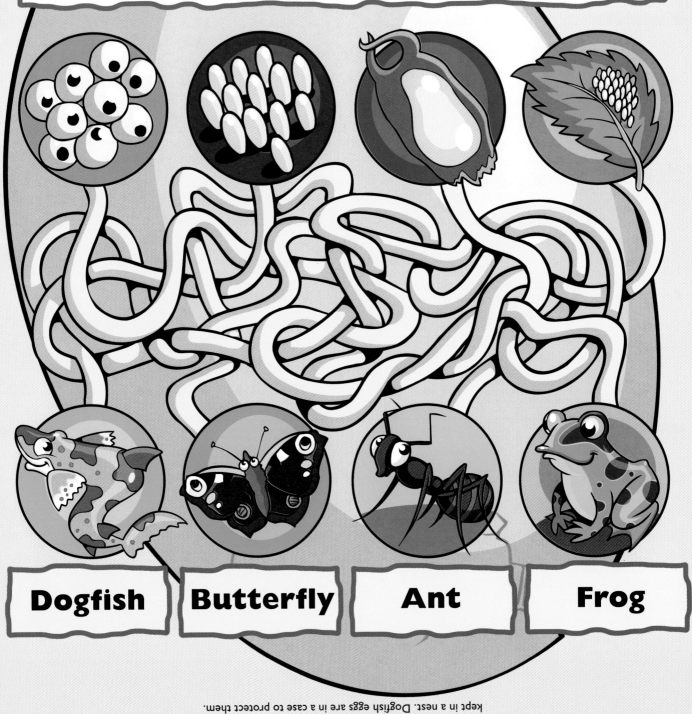

Dogfish   **Butterfly**   **Ant**   **Frog**

The Cricket who Landed in Trouble

Cricket wanted to see the Big Wide World.

"My mind is made up. I'm going to see what I can see!" he told his mother.

"My, what big ideas you've got," she said. "But don't forget to look before you leap or you might land in trouble."

He said goodbye. Then, without looking where he might land, he jumped high into the air.

Cricket landed by a pond. It was flatter and wetter than the grass where he lived. He watched a strange insect dip and dart over the water. It had a bright blue body and four wings.

"Who are you?" asked Cricket.

"I'm Dragonfly," said Dragonfly.

"My, what big eyes you've got!" said Cricket.

"All the better to see you with," said Dragonfly, looking at him as he dived and dashed about. Dragonfly didn't stay still for a minute. "And all the better to spot danger, too" he added. "You never know who will want to eat you!" And he darted off over the water.

Without looking, Cricket jumped high into the air. He landed on a leaf. It was greener and smaller than the grass where he lived. There he saw a small black insect running about.

"Who are you?" asked Cricket.

"I'm Ant," said Ant.

"My, what big feelers you've got."

"All the better to feel you with," said Ant, touching him with his big feelers. "And all the better to sense danger coming, too," he added and raced off on his way.

Without looking, Cricket jumped high into the air. He landed on a big yellow flower. It was taller and brighter than the grass where he lived.

He saw a black and yellow insect buzzing round the flower.

"Who are you?" asked Cricket.

"I'm Wasp," said Wasp.

"My, what a shiny nose you've got," said Cricket.

"All the better to smell things with," said Wasp, "and to see if they're sweet enough to eat," she added, sniffing the flower.

Without looking, Cricket jumped high into the air. He landed on an old rotten log. It was darker and damper than the grass where he lived. He heard a clicking noise from underneath.

"Who is that?" asked Cricket.

A long, shiny thing with lots of legs slithered out from under the log.

"I'm Centipede," said Centipede. "How did you know I was hiding?"

"I heard you," said Cricket.

"Ah," said Centipede. "My, what big legs you've got!"

"All the better to hear you with!" said Cricket.

"Are you trying to be clever?" snapped Centipede.

"No, I thought everybody knew that crickets have their ears in their legs!" said Cricket.

Centipede clicked his big, sharp jaws together and licked his lips.

"My, what a big mouth you've got," said Cricket.

"All the better to EAT you with!" said Centipede.

But Cricket was too quick for him. He sprang into the air and jumped all the way home.

"So what did you learn in the Big Wide World?" asked his mother.

"To look before I leap!" said Cricket, "and that not everybody knows that crickets hear with their legs."

Who's hiding here?

Join the dots to find one of the creatures Cricket found on his travels.

When you've finished drawing, colour in the picture.

A dragonfly

62

The King of All the Fishers

Heron and Kingfisher were always arguing.

"I'm the best fisher on the river," said Heron.

"No you're not. I am," said Kingfisher.

"I think you'll find," said Heron, "that I am, in fact, the best fisher in these parts."

"And I think you'll find," argued Kingfisher, "that my name is Kingfisher for a very good reason!"

"Let's ask the other river folk who's the best," said Heron.

But the animals of the riverbank were fed up with their arguing and boasting. They decided to teach Heron and Kingfisher a lesson.

"Why don't you have a fishing contest and settle it once and for all?" said Water Vole. "The one who catches the most fish by the end of the day is the winner."

Heron was pleased because he knew he'd win. Kingfisher was happy because he knew he couldn't lose.

"Do you mind if our friend joins in, too?" asked Vole.

"Who?" asked Heron.

"Me," said Otter.

"You?" gasped Heron

"You?" sneered Kingfisher.

"You're not afraid, are you?" asked Vole.

"Of course not!" muttered Heron.

"No!" agreed Kingfisher. "Somebody has to lose. It might as well be Otter."

63

The day of the fishing contest arrived. Heron chose his spot in the shallow water of the river. He was as still as a statue on his long, thin legs; his head pointed at the water, ready to spear any fish that swam too close. He could stand for hours, just waiting.

Kingfisher sat in the branch of a tree hanging over the river. The shade hid his bright feathers from the fish below. Every now and again he would dive into the water and come up with a fish in his beak.

But there was no sign of Otter.

"He's forgotten," said Heron snootily.

"Scared, more like," said Kingfisher smugly.

All day, the sun beat down until Heron was hot and stiff from standing still and Kingfisher was wet and tired from diving into the river. But neither would give up.

Just as the sun started to set, Otter arrived.

"You're too late!" cried Heron.

"You've lost!" snapped Kingfisher.

Otter just smiled and slipped into the river. In no time at all, he caught his first fish and set it on the bank.

"Impossible!" blustered Kingfisher.

"Beginner's luck!" spluttered Heron.

Then Otter caught another fish.

And another. Unlike Heron and Kingfisher, Otter didn't wait for fish to come to him. He swam after the fish and caught them in his mouth. So that's what he did. Again and again.

Soon the sun sank below the hills. It was the end of the contest.

"And the winner is…" announced Water Vole.

"Yes?" asked Heron.

"Yes, yes, yes?" said Kingfisher.

"Otter!" declared Water Vole.

Otter grinned sheepishly.

"But how?" gasped a tired Kingfisher.

"It's simple," said Otter. "Because you two have been so busy fishing and not arguing for a change, I've finally been able to get a good day's sleep. I'm as fresh as a daisy. Why, I feel like I could carry on fishing all night!" he chuckled.

"We've been tricked!" said Kingfisher and he flew off in a flurry of blue and orange.

"It's an outrage!" declared Heron. He spread his huge wings and flew off, too.

They were so embarrassed that from that day to this, Heron and Kingfisher never argued with each other ever again. And that is why the river is quiet and peaceful today.

Play time!

Kingfisher colours

Only one of these kingfishers is wearing the right colours. Can you tell which one? Look back at the last story for help!

Answer

A

B

C

Kingfisher colours: The correct answer is B.

Odd fish out!

One of these little fish is different from the others. Can you tell which one? Turn the page upside down for the answer.

1

4

6

2

5

3

Answer

7

Odd fish out: Fish number 3 is missing a fin.

Oh Dear, Roe Deer

It was summer in the wood. The sun shone down through the leaves, and little spots of sunlight danced in the shadows on the ground.

Doe Roe Deer and her two young fawns skipped happily through the trees. Doe Roe Deer had a chestnut brown coat. The Oldest Fawn had a brown coat, too. But the Littlest Fawn was different. She had silvery spots on hers.

"Oh dear," she said.

"Don't worry. You're supposed to have spots," said her mother.

Doe Roe Deer liked to eat leaves. The Oldest Fawn liked to eat leaves, too. But the Littlest Fawn was different. She still liked her mother's milk.

"Oh dear," she said.

"Don't worry. You're supposed to drink milk," said her mother.

Doe Roe Deer was hungry. The Oldest Fawn was hungry too. But the Littlest Fawn wasn't hungry at all because she'd just had some milk.

"Oh dear," she said.

"Don't worry. Lie quietly among the brambles until we come back," said her mother.

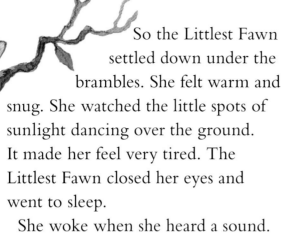

So the Littlest Fawn settled down under the brambles. She felt warm and snug. She watched the little spots of sunlight dancing over the ground. It made her feel very tired. The Littlest Fawn closed her eyes and went to sleep.

She woke when she heard a sound. She thought it was her mother and was going to call out when she saw Fox, licking his lips.

"Oh dear, oh dear," she said.

Her mother had often warned her that Fox would gobble her up if he found her.

Fox trotted across the glade.

The Littlest Fawn stayed as still as a stone.

Fox looked round the glade.

The Littlest Fawn stayed as quiet as a mouse.

Fox walked right by the brambles. Spots of sunlight danced over the bramble bush like bright silver spots. Fox walked right on past. He didn't even see her.

When Doe Roe Deer and the Oldest Fawn came back, the Littlest Fawn told them what happened.

Doe Roe Deer smiled.

"That's why you have silver spots, dear, to make you look like part of the wood and help hide you," she said.

Summer changed into autumn

and the Littlest Fawn grew into a deer. She stopped drinking milk and started to eat leaves. Her coat became thick and brown. It kept her warm but her lovely silver spots had gone.

One day, she was busy eating when she heard a sound.

It was Fox.

"Oh dear," she said. "How will I hide without my spots?"

Fox came closer and closer.

The Littlest Fawn stayed as still as a stone.

Fox looked up at her.

The Littlest Fawn looked down at him.

"Oh dear, roe deer," he sighed. "Much too big," and wandered off.

When Doe Roe Deer came back, the Littlest Fawn told her mother what had happened.

Doe Roe Deer smiled.

"You don't need your silver spots to hide you any more. You're much too big for Fox to hunt you now, dear," she said.

And the Littlest Fawn knew it was true. She didn't have to worry about Fox ever again, for she was no longer the littlest fawn.

But every now and again, when the sun shone down through the leaves, she would lie in the shade and pretend that the little spots of sunlight dancing over her fur were her very own silver spots.

Puzzle fun

Can you spot the six differences between the two pictures?

Draw a circle round each difference you spot. If you get stuck, answers are on the left of the page.

The Lonesome Pine

A young red deer loved to wander the high hills and the low glens of the Scottish highlands.

On top of the highest hills, he ate the heather.

In the lowest glens, he ate the leaves off the trees.

When he was thirsty, he drank the water from the rivers and streams.

But halfway up, neither on the top of the hills, nor at the bottom of the glen, stood a lonely old pine tree.

"What a scruffy looking thing!" said Young Deer. "It's not even a proper tree. It's got thin, shiny needles instead of flat, juicy leaves. They're tough and hard. And its horrible flaky bark tastes bitter. I can't eat this! And if I can't eat it, what good is it?"

But the old pine tree didn't mind. "I am what I am," it thought to itself, "and I'm very happy with that, thank you very much."

Every time Young Red Deer went from the high hills to the low glens or from the low glens to the high hills, he ignored the old pine tree.

But the pine tree didn't mind. "I am what I am," it thought to itself, "and I'm very happy with that, thank you very much."

Summer ended and autumn passed, the cold wind started to blow and snow began to fall.

Young Red Deer made up his mind to go down to the glen where it was safer. He was only halfway down when the wind blew so hard and the snow fell so fast that it became a snowstorm. For every step he took, the wind tried to blow Young Red Deer back. The snow swirled about him like a swarm of angry insects so that he couldn't see where he was going.

"If I don't get out of this storm I'll freeze and perish!" he cried.

Then in the blustery blizzard he saw a shape. A tall raggedy shape, standing fast against the fury of the wind. It was the old pine tree.

Cold, wet and unhappy, Young Red Deer crept under the branches of the old tree and curled up behind its thick, wide trunk. There, where the wind couldn't reach him and the snow couldn't touch him, he settled down and waited for the storm to pass.

The old pine tree didn't mind and it didn't mind the weather, either. Snow didn't stick to its shiny pine needles. It slid straight off and fell away. Under its flaky bark, its strong trunk held firm against the wind. The old pine was very happy with that, thank you very much.

By morning, the wind had died down and the snow had stopped.

Young Red Deer stood up and stretched.

"I'm glad you're not like other trees," he said. "I'm glad your leaves are tough and hard. And I'm glad your trunk is thick and strong, otherwise I would have perished. You are what you are and I'm very happy with that. Thank you very much."

Now, every time he went up to the high hills or down to the low glens, he stopped a while to rest in the shade of the old pine tree.

And the not-so-lonely old pine tree didn't mind at all.

Spot the difference

Can you see six differences between the two pictures? Circle them when you spot them.

74

The Blackbird and the Fox

Late one autumn day, Blackbird was digging in a heap of leaves for things to eat. He threw the leaves about to see what he could find under them. All sorts of creatures lived among the dead leaves that were good for a blackbird to eat. There were hard ones, soft ones, crunchy ones, slippery ones, slimy ones and stringy ones. And they were all very tasty.

"Yum," said Blackbird, as he poked his beak into the leaves to reach the juicy bugs.

Just then, Fox came by. He stopped to watch Blackbird rooting about happily in the leaves. After a while he said, "What are you doing?"

"Nothing, Fox," said Blackbird. "I'm just eating the bugs and beasties that are eating the fallen leaves, that's all."

"Well, they sound mighty tasty," said Fox, licking his lips.

"Yes," said Blackbird. "There are hard ones, soft ones, crunchy ones, slippery ones, slimy ones and stringy ones and –"

"Yes, yes," said Fox, quickly. "I'm sure they are all very tasty."

"Oh, you wouldn't like them," said Blackbird. "They're not fox food at all."

"I don't know about that," said Fox. "I eat anything."

"Anything?" said Blackbird.

"Anything," said Fox, looking at Blackbird. "So if you don't mind, I think I might try some myself when you've gone to bed."

"But if you eat them all there will be nothing left for me," said Blackbird.

"Probably not," said Fox. "I do feel very hungry."

"Well, if you must," said Blackbird with a sigh. "But whatever you do," he said, "don't eat from my special pile of leaves over there."

"I wouldn't think of it," said Fox. And off he went with his nose in the air at one end and his tail in the air at the other.

After Blackbird had gone to bed, Fox came back in the night. He nosed about in the leaves with his soft, wet nose, snuffling out the juicy bugs and

gobbling them down. All the time, he kept looking over at the big pile of leaves.

"I'll bet that's where Blackbird finds the juiciest bugs of all. That's why he didn't want me to eat from it," said Fox. "Well, he can't fool me. Nobody gets the better of Fox. Besides, I'm still hungry. I'll eat all those up, too!"

He licked his lips and stuck his nose into the big pile of leaves. He felt a painful prick on the end of his nose.

"OUCH!" he yelped. He dug into the pile with his paw.

"OUCH!" he cried again as something stung his paw.

For lying snug amongst the leaves was Hedgehog with her sharp prickles, curled up in a ball and fast asleep.

Fox's nose hurt so much and his paw throbbed so hard he had to limp all the way home. And from that day to this he never dug into a pile of leaves again – just in case.

Up in his tree, Blackbird opened a sleepy eye and grinned before going back to sleep. That would teach Fox not to be so greedy.

Who is in the wood tonight?

Minibeast maze

Can you help Blackbird find the bug? Find a route through the maze to give him a meal.

Who is in the wood tonight?

Join up the dots to find out.

Once you've joined the dots, why don't you colour in the picture?

A fox

The Mud Party

Curlew lived high above the town on the boggy peaks and moors. He was so grown up, Mother and Father Curlew no longer told him what to do.

"I can go where I want and do what I want," he said.

But all Curlew wanted to do was stay on the moors, poking his long, pointy beak in the boggy ground to look for food. He found lots of tasty beetles, grubs and caterpillars to eat.

"There's nothing finer than being on the moors with the wind in your face, the sun on your feathers and your beak in the bog," he said, with the wind in his face, the sun on his feathers and his beak in the bog.

One day, in the middle of summer, his parents said "We're leaving, son."

"Leaving?' said Curlew.

"For the mud party," they said. "Are you coming?"

Curlew didn't have to do what they said any more. So he said, "No! I'm a curlew and curlews live on the moors with the wind on their faces, the sun on their feathers and their beaks in the bog!"

"Suit yourself," said his parents as they flew off. "See you at the mud party."

"I'm not going to the mud party," he called after them. But they were gone.

"Well, I'm not going!" he said huffily.

Every now and again, he would see other curlews flying overhead.

"Are you coming to the mud party?" they called.

"No," said Curlew. "I live on the moors —"

"Yes, yes," they said. "We know; wind, sun, bog. Whatever. See you at the mud party."

"But I'm not going to the mud party!" he called, stamping his little foot in a boggy puddle.

Autumn came and it became harder to find beetles, grubs and caterpillars. One day, some of his curlew friends flew past.

"Where are you going?" he asked.

"To the mud party," they said.

"But we're curlews —" he began.

"Yes, yes. Face, feathers, beak, blah blah blah. We know," they said. "But the wind is chilly, the sun is not so warm, the bog is colder and harder on our beaks and the beetles, grubs and caterpillars have gone."

"But we can go where we want and do what we want," said Curlew.

"And we want to go to the mud party," they said, so they did.

Curlew sighed and flew into the air after his friends.

"So what's at this mud party

then?" he asked.

"Mud!" they said happily.

They all flew together down from the high peaks and moors and flew along the river until it went into the sea. And there, Curlew saw more mud than he had ever seen in his life – and he lived on the boggy moors!

Great crowds of curlews were enjoying the mud party. Mother and Father Curlew were there and so were all his friends from the moors. There were lots of other birds with long beaks too that he had never seen before.

Curlew knew all about being a curlew on the moors, with the wind in his face, the sun on his feathers and his beak in the bog. But what did he know about marshes and muddy seashores?

"Well it looks like bog," he said. "It feels like bog." He took a deep breath and stuck his long, pointy beak into the mud. Deeper and deeper. And he pulled out the biggest, juiciest worm he had ever seen in his life.

"You know, there's nothing finer than being on the moors with the wind in your face, the sun on your feathers and your beak in the bog," said Curlew happily. "Apart from going to the mud party every winter!"

Spot the Woodcocks!

Can you spot these well-hidden birds?

When the colours in the wood change in the autumn, woodcocks are hard to spot. There are six woodcocks just like this one hidden in the picture. Can you find them all?

The Moorhen and the Mud

Moorhen liked the river. It was a busy place. She swam about, meeting ducks, geese, and swans. Sometimes, for a change, she would fly over it. Sometimes, though, she liked to be by herself. One day, she found a little spot on a bank of mud, hidden among the reeds and sat down.

Nosy little Robin spied her out on the mud.

"I say, Moorhen," called Robin, from his perch over the bank. "Don't you usually paddle about on the river? What are you doing there?"

"Nothing," said Moorhen.

"Nothing?" said Robin, who couldn't believe it. "Maybe she's in trouble and too proud to ask for help," he said to himself.

"What's the matter?" said Water Vole, wandering along the bank.

"It's Moorhen," said Robin. "She's just sitting there."

"Why?" asked Water Vole. "Is she ill?"

"If I was ill, I'd fly home," said Robin. "Can you fly?" he called to Moorhen.

Moorhen sighed. "Yes, I can fly," she said. But she didn't.

"If I get into trouble I jump straight into the water," Water Vole said. "Can you do that?" he called.

"What's going on?" said Fish, hearing all the noise and swimming up to the bank to find out what was happening.

"It's Moorhen," said Robin.

"She's on the muddy bank," said Water Vole.

"Oh dear, is she stuck?" asked Fish.

"We thought she might be in a spot of trouble," said Robin.

"If I get into trouble I swim away," said Fish. "Can you swim?" she called out to Moorhen.

Moorhen sighed. "Yes, I can swim," she said. But she didn't.

Deer saw the other creatures gathered by the bank. "What's going on?" she asked.

"It's Moorhen. She's out on the mud," said Fish.

"Is she stuck?" asked Deer. "Mud can be very sticky, you know."

"Yes, we thought she might be in trouble," said Robin and Water Vole.

"If I get into trouble I just run away," said Deer. "But if I went to help her I'd just sink in the soft mud."

Moorhen sighed. She stood up on

her large feet and her long toes. "I am trying to sleep!" she said.

"We thought you were stuck in the mud!" said Robin.

"No, I wasn't," said Moorhen. "I'm a moorhen." She began to walk toward them over the mud on her big feet and long toes.

"What big feet you've got," said Water Vole.

"All the better for walking on mud without sinking," said Moorhen.

"I think we woke her up," said Robin.

"Does she look cross to you?" said Fish. "She looks cross to me."

"Yes, I think we're the ones in trouble!" said Water Vole.

"Ah," said Robin and flew away.

"Oh," said Water Vole and jumped into the river.

"Ooops!" said Fish as she swam off.

"Sorry," said Deer, running away.

"Thank goodness," said Moorhen. "Peace and quiet at last!"

She walked slowly back over the mud on her big, broad feet and settled down for a long, deep sleep.

Spotty robins

Not all robins have a red breast. When baby robins leave the nest, they have spotty feathers. They will grow red feathers to look like their parents by the autumn.

Can you put these robins in order of age from 1 to 5? Start with the spottiest first.

Do you know what these robins are looking for?

Answer: Worms

The Sign of Spring

All through winter, the shed at the bottom of the garden stood forgotten by most, but not by all.

Waiting for spring, Field Mouse made herself a nice warm nest of shredded newspaper at the bottom of an old Wellington boot in the corner, behind the rusty watering can and the old tennis rackets.

There were other creatures in the shed waiting for spring, too. There was the grumpy old spider that lived in the cracked plant pot. Then there was the thing that never said a word. It hung in the shadows above the door, its dull, grey wings folded shut.

Every day Field Mouse ran excitedly along the shed wall.

"Morning Spider. Morning thing," she said.

She peered out through a little gap into the garden, looking for any sign of spring.

"Well?" said Spider.

"Cold and wet today," she reported. "No sign of spring yet."

"Hmph!" said Spider.

On days when it was too cold to go out, Field Mouse stayed in the shed and ate the seeds and nuts she had saved from autumn.

"Well?" said Spider.

"Chilly and crisp today," she said with a shiver. "Not spring yet."

"Tut!" said Spider.

Other days, she crept out through the gap to see what seeds and nuts she could find.

"Well?" said Spider.

"Bright and windy today," she said. "No sign of spring, but it must come soon."

One day, the sunlight was strong enough to warm the shed.

Field Mouse scampered hopefully along the wall and peered out of the gap.

"Well?" said Spider.

"Bright and warm today," she said, "It might be spring, but I can't tell. There's no sign that says it really is spring," she sighed.

"Bah!" said Spider.

"Ahem!" said the thing above the door, now warmed by a beam of dusty sunlight. "I'm a sign," it said.

Field Mouse stopped and stared.

"Sorry," said Field Mouse, "but signs are bright and clear, you can't miss them. You are dull and grey. You must be mistaken."

"You're just not seeing me in the right light," said the thing.

"And what's that?" asked Field Mouse.

"Spring," it said proudly, opening up its drab, grey wings with a flourish to reveal bright, beautiful colours on the other side.

"Ta-daaa!" it said. "Is that bright and clear enough for you?"

"Oh," said Field Mouse. "You're not drab and dull at all. You're a butterfly – you're a sign of spring! There was me looking and looking for a sign and you were right there under my nose all the time!"

Butterfly fluttered round the shed to stretch his wings then slipped out through a gap in the shed door.

"Where are you going?" cried Field Mouse.

"Out!" said Butterfly. "I'm a sign of spring. Now it's here, everyone will want to see me."

Field Mouse watched him flutter off across the garden to let everyone else know.

"It's spring at last!" sighed Field Mouse happily.

"And about time, too," muttered Spider.

Dot-to-dot surprise!

Join the dots to find out who is in the middle of the page. Turn the page upside down to find out if you're not sure.

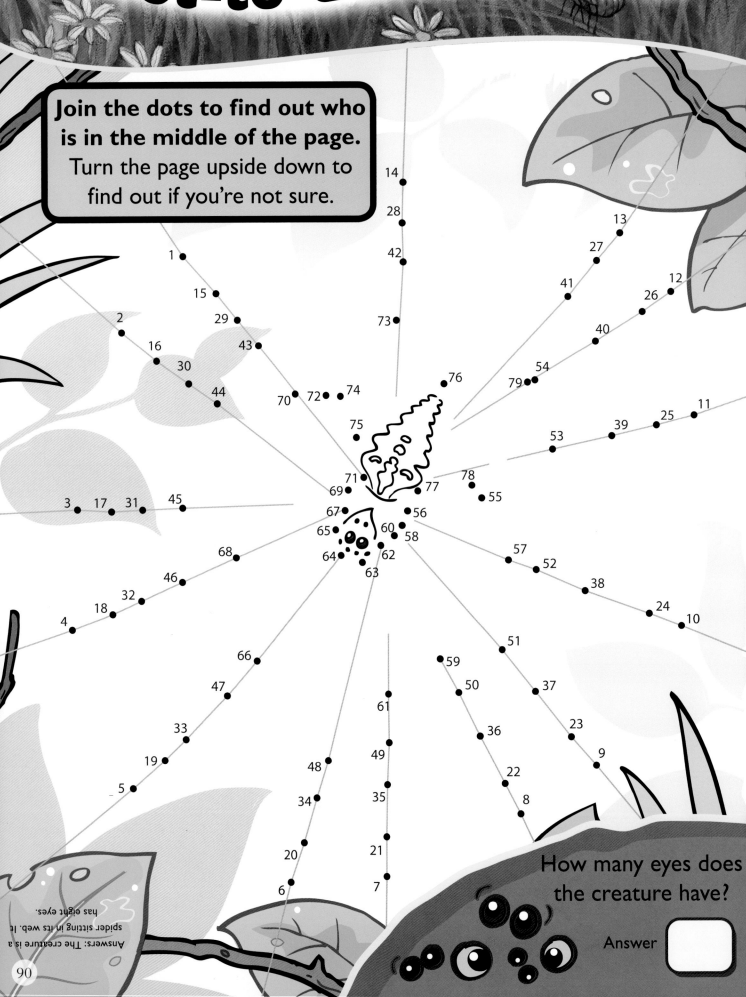

14
28
42
73
1
15
29
43
2
16
30
44
70 72 74
75
71
69 77
67
65 60
58
64 62
63
3 17 31 45
68
46
32
18
4
66
47
33
19
5
48
34
20
6
61
49
35
21
7
76
79 54
53 39 25 11
78
55
57
52
38
24 10
51
59
50 37
36 23
9
22
8
13
27
41
12
26
40

How many eyes does the creature have?

Answer

The Hole Story

Ash the tree had grown in the forest all his long life. But there were lots of younger trees there now. They made Ash feel very old indeed.

"Nobody cares about an old tree like me," he said. "I'm no use to anyone any more. I've got an old, knotty trunk, twisted branches and I have an ache in my fork," he sighed.

At the fork in his trunk, where two great branches met, rainwater had collected over the years. It soaked through the bark and made the wood soft and damp.

But some things in the forest liked old, damp wood. Fungus did and it started to grow in Ash's old, aching fork. It sent little threads, like roots, down into the damp wood.

"That tickles!" said Ash.

But as the fungus got bigger, the wood began to get softer and weaker.

"Oh!" said Ash. "I'm not sure I like this!" It was hard to hold his heavy branch up.

Then, one wild and rainy night, there was a loud crack and the branch snapped right off.

"Oh dear," said Ash. But at least the pain of holding up the heavy branch with soft, old wood was gone. Now there was just a great scar of bare wood and the beginnings of a hole.

The fungus kept growing and, as it grew, the wood became softer and started to rot.

"No one is going to want a rotten old tree like me," sighed Ash.

But the beetles did. Beetles like nice, soft wood.

"Over here!" cried a beetle.

"Is it soft? Is it damp?" asked another. It was. The crumbling, damp wood was the perfect place to lay their eggs.

When the young beetle grubs hatched, they ate the dead, damp wood, and made little tunnels as they burrowed through it. Some birds saw the damp wood too. They knew that meant beetles. Very soon, the birds were pecking at the wood to get to the lovely, juicy, beetle grubs.

"Oi!" said Ash. "Stop it!"

But as the beetle grubs tunnelled and the birds pecked, the hole got bigger. The beetle grubs turned into adults and flew away. Ash was all alone again.

Over the years the rain fell. Beetles returned. Grubs tunnelled and birds pecked.

The hole grew bigger.

Ash got quite used to having a hole. He was never quite sure what would happen to it next.

One year, a female great tit spied

the hollow.

"That's almost right for a nest," she said. She chipped out a few more bits of wood to make it a little bigger. "There. Perfect!" She lined it with grass and moss and sheep's wool and animal hair. Then she laid her seven eggs.

Ash was as excited as a tree could be waiting for the eggs to hatch. When they did, there were seven cheeping chicks snuggled in his hole.

But by the end of the summer, the chicks had grown up and were gone. The hole was empty again and Ash was all alone once more.

Summer turned to autumn and the nights became colder.

Ash felt a little fluttering deep inside. It was a little wren and it had

found the hole.

"Ooh," said the wren. "I must tell the others!" So it did.

That night, five or six wrens all huddled together in the hole. They kept each other dry and warm through the cold, dark night. And they slept there every night for the whole winter.

"Perhaps I'm not so old and useless after all," said Ash happily.

It was true.

An old tree with a hole was very important in the forest. Think of all the creatures that needed it!

Bedtime for birds

Help the wrens find their tree hole for the night.

Wrens sleep together in nestboxes when it's cold. Once, 63 wrens were found in the same nestbox!

More for You

The stories in this book first appeared in **Wild Times**, the RSPB magazine for under 8s. You can read more stories and follow the adventures of Red, Rookie, Owlbert and Squeak by joining RSPB Wildlife Explorers.

As a member, you'll receive **Wild Times** six times a year, be able to take part in competitions and projects, go to nature reserves and know that you are helping to protect wildlife.

Visit the world's biggest wildlife club for children at:
www.rspb.org.uk/youth

Pat Kelleher is a freelance writer with many magazine, radio and animation credits to his name. He has also published several children's non-fiction and fiction titles, including the acclaimed *No Man's World* adventure series for young adults. His passion for nature has led him to become the RSPB's storyteller of choice for their youth magazine, **Wild Times**, from which the stories for this compendium were selected.

Daniel Howarth is a published author and illustrator of over 30 children's books. He collaborated with Pat Kelleher on illustrating stories for the RSPB's **Wild Times** magazine for over six years, and his fantastic work can be seen illustrating Pat's stories throughout this book.

Games and activity illustrations were provided by **Ian Claxton** and **Anthony Rule**.